For Aimee, Aileen and Dawn · S.R.
For Katie, Jonny, Sophie and Amy · S.A.L.

MYRIAD BOOKS LIMITED
35 Bishopsthorpe Road, London SE26 4PA

First published in 1997 by
FRANCES LINCOLN LIMITED
4 Torriano Mews, Torriano Avenue, London NW5 2RZ

ISBN 1 84746 007 0

EAN 9 781 84746 007 3

Printed in China

Best of Friends!

Shen Roddie

Illustrated by Sally Anne Lambert

MYRIAD BOOKS LIMITED

Hippo and Pig were neighbours. They lived
in a winding lane with a tall green hedge
between their houses.

On Mondays, Wednesdays and Fridays,
Hippo waddled over to Pig's house for
peppermint tea and chocolate doughnuts.

On Tuesdays, Thursdays and Saturdays,
Pig trotted over to Hippo's for a cool mud-bath.

One Sunday, the day when they stayed at home,
Pig decided to knit Hippo a scarf.

   "It'll be finished just in time for his birthday,"
said Pig, and started to knit.

That same Sunday, Hippo decided to do something nice and neighbourly for Pig.

"I'll cut down the hedge between us," he thought. "Then we can see into each other's houses and really be friends." He got out his shears, climbed up a ladder and began to clip the hedge.

"SNIP, SNIP, SNIP!" went
the shears.

"WOBBLE, WOBBLE, WOBBLE!"
went the ladder.

The tall green hedge got shorter and shorter.

"Wallowing walruses!" exclaimed Hippo,
peering over the hedge. "I can see Pig in her
house. She's knitting a scarf. I bet it's a present
for my birthday!"

Hippo hurried into his house.
"I'd better make a present for Pig," he said,
and he got out his modelling clay.

Just then, Pig looked up from her knitting.

"Fluttering flamingos!" exclaimed Pig.
"The hedge has shrunk!"
Pig stared right into Hippo's house.
"He's making a mug with a pig on it.
I'm sure it's a present for my birthday!"

As Pig watched, Hippo waddled into another
room and flopped on to a settee. He started
chewing his toe-nails - all sixteen of them.
"Revolting!" thought Pig.

Then Hippo went off to cook lunch.
As he cooked, he kept licking the ladle
and putting it back in the pot.

"UGH!" shrieked Pig in horror,
as she thought of all the bowls of soup
she had drunk at Hippo's house.

Pig had seen quite enough. She needed a snack.
Hippo looked up and saw Pig through the window.
As he watched, Pig pounced on a pile of cream buns . . .

. . . and stuffed them all down in one go!
It made Hippo feel sick.

"Time for some exercise," said Pig,
belching loudly.

"Dancing is *very* good exercise,"
said Pig, as she sucked in her breath
to button her tutu.

She whirled, and she twirled,
then . . .

SNAP! The tutu burst and Pig
fell flat on her face.

Hippo roared with laughter. He had
never seen Pig look so funny.

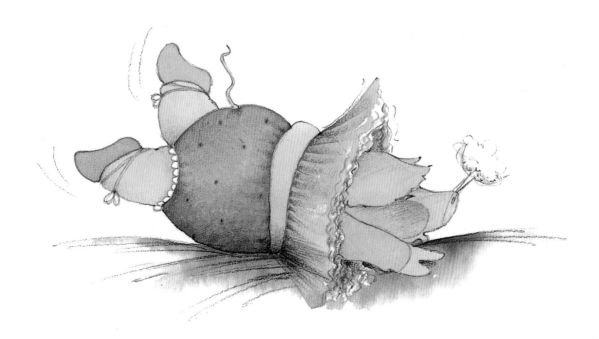

Pig heard Hippo chuckling and looked out of her
window.

"Hippo!" shouted Pig. "Are you watching me?"

"Yes, Pig!" answered Hippo. "You were gorging
cream buns and falling flat on your face."

Pig blushed.

"Well," she said, "you were chewing your
toe-nails and licking your soup ladle."

"YOU WERE WATCHING ME!" they cried.
"NO I WASN'T!" they shouted.
"YES YOU WERE!" they yelled.

Pig drew her pink curtains.
Hippo pulled down his green blinds.

After that, Pig and Hippo stopped seeing each other.

Every day, Pig drank peppermint tea alone in her garden . . .

Every day, Hippo took
a mud-bath all by himself.
Meanwhile, the hedge
grew back tall and green.

At last, it was Hippo's birthday.

Pig picked up the scarf she had knitted
and crept over to Hippo's house.

"Happy birthday, Hippo!" she said shyly.

"Oh Pig, what a *lovely* surprise. Thank you,"
Hippo said, as he unwrapped the scarf. "I have
a present for you, too, but you'll have to wait
until *your* birthday. You'll never guess what it is!"

They both laughed . . .

And as it was a Monday, Hippo went back
to Pig's house for peppermint tea, chocolate
doughnuts and a special iced cake.

Pig and Hippo were the best of friends again.
But ever after, back in their own homes . . .

. . . they did . . .

exactly as they pleased!